# The Big Tree Mouse Adventure

## Martin Waddell
## Illustrated by Wilbert van der Steen

This is Little and Small and No-Size-At-All before their Great Tree Mouse Adventure.

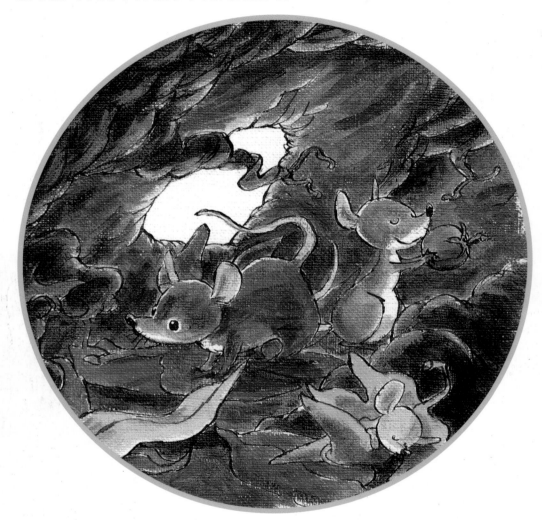

The three mice lived under the roots of a tree in a large wood. They were safely hidden under their tree until, one day, the roots shook and . . .

# CRASH!

Down came their tree and all the other trees
in the wood.

# Somehow . . .

. . . they escaped, but when they came out, their whole world had gone.

"We've got to leave here right now," Small told Little.

So the three mice set out on their journey to find a new home. Small and Little took turns to carry No-Size-At-All because No-Size-At-All was too tiny to walk very far.

There were broken roots and big boots and machines all around them.

"Where shall we go?" Little squeaked.

"We'll go this way," decided Small.

But they didn't get very far before they came to . . .

# a raging hot fire!

Somehow . . .

   . . .  they escaped through the flames and the smoke, though their tails and their whiskers were singed.

When the three mice had recovered, they started
walking again.

"Which way shall we go?" Little squeaked.

"This way!" said Small, though she didn't really know
where to go.

*Someone* had to decide, so Small did.

# Somehow . . .

. . . they escaped, though Little got scratched and
Small almost lost the tip of her tail.

"Which way now?" Little asked Small.

"I don't know," said Small.

So Little climbed up a broken fence post, and then . . . the moon rose.

"I can see tree tops far away!" Little squeaked.
"Then that's where we're going," said Small.

Little and Small took turns carrying No-Size-At-All.
Sometimes the tiny mouse walked by himself, though
his short legs couldn't go very fast.

On and on they walked, past an old shoe, across
some stones, over a log, down one side of a ditch and
up the other.

"I can't walk much further," Little squeaked.
"We **have** to go on," Small told Little.

They went on and on, on and on, on and on.

And then . . .

"**TREES!**" gasped No-Size-At-All.

At last, the three mice had reached the end of their journey.

The mice searched among the tree roots for
somewhere to make their new home.

"This one?" said Little.

"That one?" said Small.

But it was No-Size-At-All who found the best place,
where the tree roots were just right for small mice
to dig.